Sleepy Bird

JEREMY TANKARD

Scholastic Press
New York

It was
bedtime.
But Bird
was not
ready
to go
to sleep.

His wings wanted to flap.
His legs wanted to run.
All of him wanted to play.

"WHEE!" said Bird.

"It's party time!"

Fox was getting cozy
when he heard Bird coming.
"Goodness," said Fox. "That's
a lot of noise for bedtime!"
"I'm not tired," said Bird.

"Maybe if you hugged my blankie," said Fox. "It helps me get sleepy."

"Blankie shmankie," said Bird. "Let's play!"

Fox was too sleepy to play.
So Bird went to find Beaver.

"It's bedtime, Bird," said Beaver.

"Bedtime is for babies," said Bird.

"How about I read you a story?" said Beaver.

"How about you don't," said Bird.

He tapped Beaver on the arm.

"Tag, you're it!"

**Bird ran to Rabbit's house,
but Beaver didn't follow.**

"Everybody says it's bedtime," said Bird, "but I'm not tired."

"Want to snuggle my stuffed kitty?" asked Rabbit.

"A STUFFED CAT?!" said Bird.

"Are you TRYING to give me nightmares?"

Bird went to find Raccoon.
"Raccoon," said Bird, "you'll play with me, right?"
"It's bedtime," said Raccoon. "I'm going to sing a soft lullaby and drift off to sleep."

"But you're NOCTURNAL!" said Bird.

"Why won't anyone play?"

Bird flounced over to Sheep's place.

"You know what you need?" said Sheep.
"New friends?" suggested Bird.
"You need to count sheep," said Sheep.
"That always helps me fall asleep."

"BUT THERE'S ONLY ONE OF YOU!" shouted Bird.

"HOW CAN YOU GET SLEEPY COUNTING TO *ONE*?!"

Bird stormed off.

If no one would play with him, he would just walk forever.

After a little while, his wings drooped. His legs crumpled.

"I AM NOT TIRED!" he cried.

"WHY SHOULD I

GO TO SLEEP?"

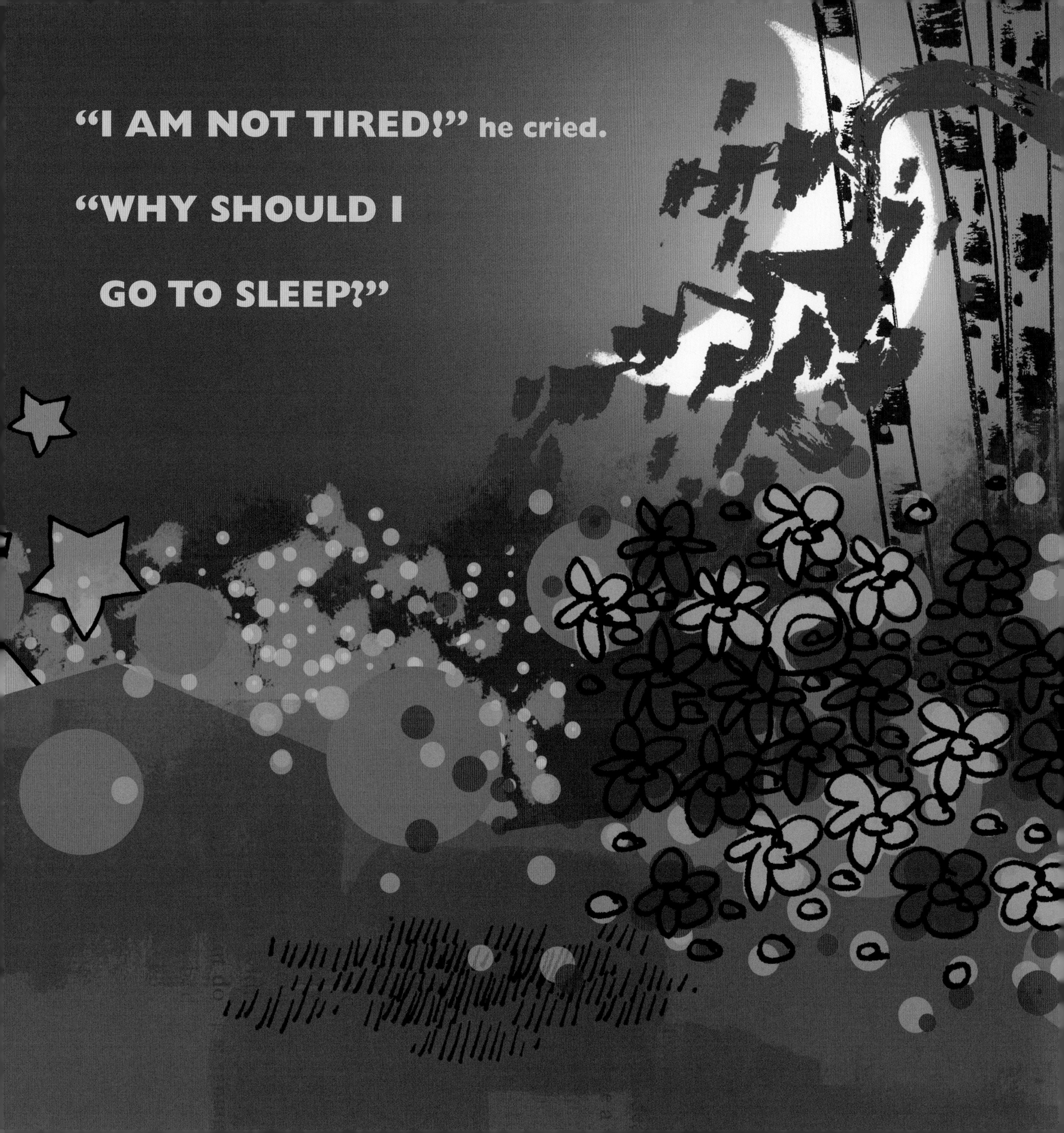

Bird's friends heard his cries
and came running.

Fox covered Bird with his blankie.
Beaver read a story.
Rabbit tucked his stuffed kitty under Bird's wing.
Raccoon sang a quiet song.
Sheep counted herself until she got to
one more times than she could count.

"I . . . Am . . . Not . . . Sleeeepy . . ."
mumbled Bird as his eyes closed.

"Finally," said his friends.

"I thought he'd NEVER fall asleep," said Fox.

They lay down near Bird and slept.

Bird rolled over.
He opened his eyes.
He yawned
and stretched.

"Hiya!" chirped Bird.

"Who wants to play?"